Some children have lots of siblings.

Some children have none.

Some children have two dads.

Some have one mom.

Some children live with their grandparents . . .

and some live with an aunt.

Some children have many pets . . .

and some just have a plant!

Some children live with their father.

Some children have two mothers.

Some children are adopted.

Some have stepsisters and—brothers.

Some children bunk with their cousins.

Some have a mom and a pop.

Some children's parents are married.

Some children's parents are not.

So no matter if you have

a ma,

a pa,

a hog,

this llama,

ten frogs and a slug,

a cousin named Doug,

a Great-Grandma Betty
and a Great-Aunt Sue,

Uncles Hal,
Al, and Sal,
and Uncle Lou, too,

one stepsis, three stepbros,
two stepmoms, and a prize-winning rose,

a robot butler
to serve you tea,

the world's biggest grandpa,

or whatever it might be . . .

. . . if you love each other,
then you are a family.